ALSO BY STEPHEN ROOS

THIRTEENTH SUMMER

Thirteenth Summer

by Stephen Roos

Illustrations by Dee deRosa

Atheneum   1987   New York

Atheneum
Macmillan Publishing Company
866 Third Avenue, New York, NY 10022
Collier Macmillan Canada, Inc.

Type set by Haddon Craftsmen, Allentown, Pennsylvania
Printed and bound by Fairfield Graphics, Fairfield, Pennsylvania
Designed by Marjorie Zaum
First Edition

10 9 8 7 6 5 4 3 2 1

Library of Congress Cataloging–in–Publication Data

Roos, Stephen.
Thirteenth summer.

SUMMARY: A fight with his best friend Mackie,
one of the wealthy summer people who live part-time
on his island, starts thirteen–year–old Pink wondering
if they are envious of each other and if he himself
really wants to go to school on the mainland.
[1. Islands—Fiction. 2. Friendship—Fiction]
I. DeRosa, Dee, ill. II. Title.
PZ7.R6753Th   1987   [Fic]   87-11382
ISBN 0-689-31299-7

For Larry Stoddard

THIRTEENTH SUMMER

1

PINK STOOD at the edge of the sea watching the gulls soar and swoop above the waves. Their screeching was almost hideous, but their antics were comical. He chuckled as one of the gulls dove into the water, splashed along the surface, and soared back into the sky with a silvery fish in its beak.

Pink remembered that he would be having fish for dinner too. His mother had promised a mariner's stew for supper that night. With gulls to laugh at and a mariner's stew to look forward to, he wondered why some things were getting to him this summer, things that had never bothered him before.

"Pink?"

Phoebe was calling from the steps along the bluff, but he didn't turn around. He picked up the rake that lay on the sand and pretended he hadn't heard her. It wasn't nice but he did it anyway. Phoebe Wilson was one of the things that bothered him the most this summer.

With both hands gripped firmly on the handle, Pink raked the dark green, almost black seaweed into a pile. Phoebe's mother used it as mulch for her flowers. She claimed that the nutrients in Plymouth Island seaweed made her delphiniums the most beautiful along the entire New England coast. This summer Pink was part-time assistant to the Wilsons' gardener. He wondered if Mrs. Wilson ever gave credit to the gardener who planted the flowers in the spring and weeded, watered, and mulched them throughout the summer, but he didn't wonder long. Phoebe's voice was too insistent for him to concentrate.

"Didn't you hear me?" she asked. "I was calling you, Pink."

Pink let the rake fall onto the sand as he turned toward her. Even if he didn't like her anymore, he had to admit that Phoebe Wilson was a good-looking girl. Beautiful black hair that came down to her shoulders, nice hazel eyes, and a nice smile when she smiled. She was a little tall for twelve, but that was okay because he was a little tall for thirteen. They

would have made a pretty good-looking couple, he decided. It was too bad that he was never going to go out with her.

"I'm working," he said. "I want to get this mess raked up before the tide comes in."

"You can take a little break, can't you?"

"If you say so. You're the boss."

"I'm not and I don't like your talking like that," she said.

"I'll talk the way I think," he said, "and I'll think the way I please." He picked up the rake and made another stab at the seaweed.

"Aren't you going to give me a chance to apologize?" she asked. "I know what I did was wrong. Really, Pink. I feel horrible about it."

"What happened happened," Pink said. "Forget it."

"I wish I could," Phoebe said. "But I can't. I invited you to a dance and then I uninvited you when Derek Malloy asked me. I didn't mean to hurt you, but I did, and I wish there was some way to make it up to you."

"Don't try," he said. "Why should you go to some fancy yacht club dance with some island hick when you can go with an off-islander?"

Phoebe stepped back and he saw her nervous smile turn into a small pout. "Please, Pink," she sighed.

"You dumped me," Pink said. "How do you expect me to feel, Phoebe?"

"Every bit as bad as I do," she said contritely. "I feel humiliated that Kit Malloy paid her brother to invite me. But I feel worse about what I did to you. Why won't you forgive me?"

"It doesn't matter," Pink said. "You and I probably wouldn't be real friends anyway, no matter how many dances we went to."

Phoebe opened her mouth but no words came out. She shrugged and turned away. Pink watched her walk across the beach to the stairs that led up the bluff. If he had been as together as he usually was, he would have accepted her apology and all but forgotten the whole incident. But this time, he didn't know how to let the bad feeling go.

He watched Phoebe disappear into the massive gray-shingled house that stood at the edge of the bluff. Her world was a mansion in Philadelphia the rest of the year. It was a fancy private school and servants and, as Pink was quick to remind himself, servants who had servants.

Pink's world was Plymouth Island all year round. It was his father's boatyard and the cottage on Dock Street with his mom and dad and Plymouth Regional, where there were only nine other students in the eighth grade.

Phoebe said she liked him, maybe she even meant it, but she had treated him as though he didn't count. Pink wanted to blame Phoebe's world as much as Phoebe herself, but he knew he couldn't. Mackie Vanderbeck was from the same world as Phoebe but he was never like that. He always made Pink feel like he counted.

Pink raked more seaweed beyond the reach of the incoming tide. Then he climbed the stairs and put the rake in the gardener's shed next to the Wilsons' three-car garage. A moment later he was biking past the other magnificent houses that stood on the bluff looking out to sea.

Of all the months, July was usually Pink's favorite. The houses that had been boarded up for the winter were open now, there were people everywhere, and the weather was perfect. In a lot of ways, July wasn't so different from August on Plymouth Island, but even so Pink liked it better. August was closer to Labor Day when the summer people boarded up their houses and left the island.

Summer people got Pink's father hot under the collar, even though they supplied the Cunningham Boatyard with most of its business. His father didn't like how they clogged the street with their mopeds. Some of them dropped their ice cream and candy wrappers in the middle of Commercial Street. Some of them were downright slobs and yet they had the nerve to call the islanders "natives" in a way that suggested they were a lower order of Homo sapiens.

In some ways Pink agreed with his father. He wouldn't care if Phoebe took the next boat to the mainland, but on the other hand he knew Plymouth Island could be very lonely for him without the off-islanders, Mackie Vanderbeck especially. Mackie was the most regular kid he knew.

Closer to town were the houses where most of the year-rounders lived. Pink felt more comfortable there. He knew the people and they knew him. If the houses weren't as impressive as the mansions on the sea, they were still pretty and well-cared for, with tidy lawns and tall, shady elm trees in the yards.

Before arriving at his house, Pink stopped suddenly in front of a one-story bungalow with dark brown shingles—the Silvas' house. The privet hedge that separated the sidewalk from the front yard bloomed with hundreds of tiny white flowers. Bees, perhaps a thousand of them, sent out a low, persistent hum as they hovered in and around it.

Josh Silva was in Pink's class at Plymouth

Regional. They were friends, but once the summer got going, they didn't see much of each other. Now, something about the Silvas' house caught Pink's attention, something he hadn't noticed before. It wasn't the hum of the bees. Nor was it the sweet, sticky smell of the flowers. Pink got off his bike and looked again. The difference was the "For Sale" sign on the Silvas' front lawn.

Had the Silvas' put their house on the market? Pink hoped not. Although he and Josh got preoccupied during the summer, they were friends just the same.

Pink knocked three times on the frame of the screen door. He heard someone turn off the television set and move toward the door. It was Josh. He was shorter than Pink but about the same height as the rest of the kids his and Pink's age. He had short black hair, almost a crew cut.

"How you doing, Pink?" Josh asked as he stepped onto the porch.

"I'm okay," Pink said. "Tired from work. How about you? I just saw the sign. What's going on?"

"We're moving," Josh said.

"To another part of the island?" Pink asked. "Getting a bigger house?"

"We're moving to the mainland," Josh said. "In September even if the house isn't sold.

"How do you feel about it?" Pink asked.

"I don't know if I'm excited or sad."

"You're probably both," Pink said. "But I'm sorry you're moving."

"My dad says it's too hard being a fisherman. He already has a job lined up on the mainland. We're not going to be rich or anything, but we're going to be more secure. We won't have to wait around for the fish to jump into the nets."

"So it'll be better for your dad," Pink said. "How about you and your sister?"

"My dad says the mainland will be better for all of us," Josh said. "Not just him."

"There's no place better than Plymouth Island as far as I'm concerned," Pink said stiffly.

"My dad says the schools are better on the mainland," Josh said. "They have lots of things that Plymouth Regional is never going to have. Plymouth is small. My dad says it's too isolated. In the winter, there's hardly anything to do. In the summer, he complains there's too much."

"I'll agree about the summer," Pink said. "It seems like I'm working all the time. My job at the boatyard in the mornings and a couple of afternoons a week over at the Wilsons' keep me busy enough. I've got hardly enough time to go out sailing."

"I saw you in your skiff a couple of weeks ago," Josh said. "With the Wilson girl."

For a moment, Pink wondered if Josh were teasing him. "I'm not seeing Phoebe Wilson anymore," he said. "She's just summer people."

"Well, maybe my family will come back in the summer," Josh said. "You never know. Maybe I'll be one of the summer people."

"Whatever happens you'll be you," Pink said. "You'll be okay. In some ways I'm happy for you. Really. Things work out for the best, they say. Keep me posted."

Pink walked down the porch steps, got on his bike, and pedaled toward Dock Street. He was still thinking about Josh when he got up-stairs to his room and plopped down on his bed. He wasn't sleepy, but he was tired. He needed a nap.

He kicked off his sneakers and put his hands under his head. He looked across the room to the soundings map of Plymouth Island. Concentrating on it always helped Pink drift off. Soon his eyelids began to droop.

He was thinking about Josh. New place to live, new friends, new school. Pink wondered what Josh's new school would be like. Would it have hundreds of kids and an auditorium and a science lab with state-of-the-art equipment? He made a mental note to stop by Josh's house again soon. Then he looked again at the soundings map. In a moment he was asleep.

It was the first day in two weeks that Pink had forgotten to check the mail before his mom did.

2

WHEN PINK WOKE UP, the sun was just beginning to go down. Midsummer days on Plymouth Island were long ones, and after the sunset, the sky glowed 'til almost nine.

At twilight, Plymouth was still, no cars or mopeds on the streets, no lawnmowers next door or sawing and hammering from the Cunningham Boatyard. The peacefulness of the early evening usually rubbed off on Pink. Islanders and off-islanders alike agreed it was the best time of the day.

From his room, Pink could hear his mother downstairs in the kitchen. In the summer, Pink's father worked late and the Cunninghams ate later than most folks. Pink was always ravenous by suppertime. He remembered the mariner's stew. That made him hungrier than usual.

Pink got off his bed and slipped on his sneakers. He checked himself out in the mirror and ran a brush through his hair. Pink's real name was Charles Cunningham, Jr., but he had lived with the name Pink for thirteen years. It struck him as kind of dumb but he had to admit it fit. The hours of working outside in the hot summer sun had turned his usually dark red hair a shade of pink.

In the winter he usually had some freckles too, but in the summer they gradually melted into a tan. For the last year, Pink had tried to figure out if he were really good-looking or just pretty good-looking. He hadn't come to a definite decision, but for now he had settled for attractive.

He pulled on his green sweater and pushed the brush through his hair again before walking downstairs. On one side of the front hall was a living room and on the other side was a small dining room. The rooms were hardly ever used because the Cunninghams did their living and their dining in the kitchen at the back of the house.

His mother liked the kitchen because of all the sun it got. His father liked the view of Plymouth Harbor and Pink liked the way the room smelled. His mother was a terrific cook and the kitchen smelled wonderful most of the time.

As he walked into the kitchen, he saw his mother dropping codfish steaks into a steaming copper kettle. She was beautiful, Pink thought, with her sharp blue eyes, blonde hair, and no-freckle complexion. If Pink had inherited his looks from his mother rather than from his father, he wouldn't have to wonder if he were good-looking. He would just know.

"How long 'til we eat?" he asked.

"Ten minutes," his mother said. "Fifteen maybe. As soon as your father gets home."

"He's still at it?" Pink asked.

"He had to go over some accounts," his mother said. She passed him the soft Portuguese bread they ate with almost every meal. More than a century ago, men from Portugal had sailed with the New England whaling ships and many had settled on Plymouth Island. Their bread had become a Plymouth Island staple.

"Dad works too hard," Pink said. He tore a piece of bread from the loaf and bit into it.

"It's rough in the summer but he likes it that way, Pink," his mother said.

"You work too hard too," Pink said.

"I work just hard enough, Pink Cunningham," she said. "I like it at the bank. Besides, I like being solvent. So does your father. Aren't you proud to have two such fine influences around?"

At last Pink saw his father walking up the brick path that led from his office at the Boatyard. Charles Cunningham, Sr. was a tall man and most of the time he held an unlighted pipe between his teeth. Although his hair was dark brown now, it had been red years before. Pink knew where his looks came from without asking.

Charlie Cunningham let the screen door slam behind him. His kissed Pink's mother on the cheek and nodded to Pink. He sat down at the table, ready for dinner even if dinner wasn't quite ready for him.

"Four minutes, Charlie," Pink's mother said. "Don't hold your breath."

"Don't hurry on my account, Maggie," Pink's father said. He picked up a soup spoon and began to toy with it. "What were you up to this afternoon, Pink?" he asked.

"Raked some seaweed." Pink said. "Over at the Wilsons ."

"Still having problems with that girl?" his father asked.

"Her name's Phoebe," Pink's mother said.

17

"And I'm not having trouble with her," Pink said.

"You could have fooled me," his father said.

"So she dumped me for Derek Malloy," Pink said. "What's the big deal?"

"You mean that?" his mother asked cautiously.

"Why shouldn't I?"

"Sorry, Pink."

His father stuck the pipe in the breast pocket of his shirt. "That girl ever apologize to you?" he asked.

"Phoebe," Pink's mother said. "She has a name, Charlie."

"She tried," Pink said.

"You accept?"

"Not in so many words," Pink said, stiffening a bit.

"Yes or no?"

"No, I guess," Pink said. "It doesn't matter to her anyway. She thinks I'm some sort of dumb native."

"She tell you that?"

"She dumped me for Derek Malloy, Dad."

Pink was sitting next to his father. His mother carried the copper pot to the table and rested it on a straw mat at the center. She scooped up the stew into bowls and passed them around. It wasn't fancy food, but it was the best Pink had ever tasted. Pink grabbed the loaf of Portuguese bread and tore off another piece of it. He stuck the bread into the stew and tried to concentrate on satisfying his appetite instead of on Phoebe.

"The Silvas' place is for sale," he said, trying to change the subject.

"You know that for sure?" his father asked, suddenly looking upset.

"Josh told me this afternoon," Pink said. "The 'For Sale' sign is up and they're moving to the mainland after Labor Day."

"They're going to be sorry," his father said. "Mighty sorry."

His mother took a taste of her stew and rested the spoon beside her bowl. "You don't know that, Charlie."

"It's folks like us and the Silvas who make Plymouth what it is. If more of us move over, this island is going to be nothing but summer people. We've got to think of the island."

"The Silvas have to think of themselves and their children," Mrs. Cunningham said.

"It's a good life here," Mr. Cunningham said. "For them and their children."

"If they think it will be better on the mainland," Pink's mother said, "that's all that matters."

"We got all we need right here on Plymouth," Mr. Cunningham said. "We've got everything. Work, friends, and there's no place more beautiful. Right, Pink?"

"Right," Pink said uncomfortably. "But Mr. Silva says there's going to be steady work for him there."

"Well, we don't have to worry about that," Charlie said. "We got the boatyard. It's what my father wanted for me. It's what I want for you, Pink."

"*If* Pink wants it for himself," Pink's mother said. Although she hadn't finished her stew, she pushed her bowl slightly away from her.

"I don't have to decide the rest of my life right now, do I?" Pink asked.

"Of course you don't," his father said. "But you love Plymouth. You love the boatyard. Why would you ever want to go someplace else?"

"Pink?" his mother asked. "You taking all that in?"

"Yes, Mom."

"Whatever you do is your decision," she said. "It doesn't matter what your father and I want."

"But Dad's right," Pink said. "I love Plymouth. It's just that I don't have anyplace to compare it with. I've never lived anyplace else."

"Be grateful for that," his father said. "We're fine here. And if it's good enough for us, why not for the Silvas?"

Pink took one last spoonful of his stew. There was more left in the bowl, but for once the stew had outlasted his appetite. He carried the bowl to the sink. While he was rinsing it under the cold water, he became more uneasy. He remembered again that he had forgotten to check the mail that afternoon.

"Was there any mail for me today, Mom?" he asked.

"You waiting for something in particular?" she asked.

"Please, Mom. Was there anything in the mail today?"

His mother shook her head. A definite wave of relief passed through Pink's body. He would have to be more careful about getting to the mailbox from now on. He would also have to stop asking his mother about the mail. If he kept it up, she was bound to get suspicious.

"You enter one of those contests?" she asked.

"If you win a trailer home, you can give it

to the Silvas," his father said gleefully. "They may need one when they get to the mainland."

Feeling uncomfortable, Pink let himself out of the kitchen door and walked down to the pier to watch the last light fade from the sky. He saw the great orange glow from the lighthouse at the end of the point and the boats at anchor, bobbing in the harbor. When the Island's beauty was as overwhelming as it was now, Pink knew that his father was right. Who needed a mansion in Philadelphia or bigger schools or more "opportunity?" Then again, his mother had a point. What's right for one person may not be right for another.

Standing on the pier, watching night settle over the harbor, Pink thought he knew what was right, what was best for himself. Even so, tomorrow he would remember the mailbox.

3

PINK SPENT the next morning at his father's boatyard, caulking and priming the hull of a sloop. When the others broke for lunch, Pink took off for the day. He fixed himself a sandwich at home and decided to put off raking the Wilsons' beach for another day. He wasn't up to dealing with Phoebe again.

He got his bike from the shed next to the kitchen and rode along Dock Street to Commercial Street. The boutiques there were filled with fancy shirts and blouses and designer jeans that no one who lived year-round on Plymouth Island would ever wear, even if they could afford them.

Plymouth Islanders ordered most of their clothes from mail-order stores on the mainland.

In the fall, the elegant shops and high-priced restaurants on Commercial Street would close and life would revolve around the post office and the hardware store. Pink reminded himself that come September maybe his mood would be back to normal just as the Island got back to normal too.

He rode through the snarl of cars, tour buses, and pedestrians. A few blocks out, however, the traffic diminished except for a couple of mopeds, an occasional car, and some teenagers with surfboards who were thumbing rides to the other side of the island where the ocean waves broke on the unprotected shore.

A little farther out of town, Pink turned in at the Vanderbecks' house. At one time the driveway had been elegantly graveled and tended, but now it was mostly sand with a spit of grass in the middle.

The Vanderbecks' house was as large as the Wilsons' but it didn't have the word *mansion* written all over it. For one thing, it wasn't on the sea. For another thing, the Vanderbecks didn't have it painted every two years as a matter of course. Their place was painted after it looked like it needed some paint. The hedge in front was trimmed in the fall, but it wasn't manicured through the summer as the Wilsons' hedge was. The Vanderbecks had money but they didn't make a show of it. That made the whole Vanderbeck family a lot more tolerable as far as the year-rounders were concerned.

"Hey, Pink!"

Pink recognized Mackie's shout but he couldn't tell where the shout was coming from. There was no sign of Mackie, or anyone else for that matter, on the lawn or the driveway or the front porch. Pink turned full-circle to double-check.

"I'm up here," Mackie shouted. "In the attic. Come on up!"

Pink looked up. There, hanging out a dormer window on the third floor of the house, was Mackie. Even though Pink couldn't see Mackie's face clearly, he could make out the mop of blonde hair that was almost white from the summer sun.

Pink waved and ran up the porch steps to the front door. At the Vanderbecks' he didn't have to knock. He let the screen door slam behind him and bounded up the first flight of stairs. On the second floor were the Vander-becks' bedrooms. A college girl who came in twice a week to clean was vacuuming a bedroom at the front of the house. Pink nodded to her even though she was too intent on a rug to notice him. He rounded another corner and went up the last flight of stairs to the attic.

The naked light bulb hanging from the center of the ceiling was on but it didn't help much. Nor did the daylight coming through the dormer windows. Pink could barely see the trunks and cartons, the discarded chairs and lamps that were so worn out they deserved to be in the town dump instead of the Vanderbecks' attic.

At the far end of the attic, in the light of a dormer window, was Mackie. But all Pink could see were Mackie's legs and part of Mackie's back. Most of Mackie was leaning into an enormous steamer trunk.

"Mackie?" Pink asked because he still wasn't absolutely sure.

Mackie stood up and turned toward Pink. He had squarish features and very blue eyes. He would have been better looking if he had lost fifteen pounds of leftover baby fat. While Mackie waited for a power greater than his appetite to remove his excess poundage, Pink was waiting for his hair to turn brown. Their hopes about changing what they didn't much like about themselves had been one of the early bonds of their friendship.

"What do you think?" Mackie asked as he

pulled something Pink didn't recognize from the trunk and held it up for him to see.

"If you tell me what it is, I'll tell you what I think," Pink said.

"It's a lantern," Mackie said. "When it's hung up and there's a candle in it, it'll look more like one."

Pink stepped closer. Even in the poor light, he could see the intricate flowers on it—bright red peonies—against a black background. It was beautiful and very, very delicate. Pink touched it. The silk felt as beautiful and delicate as it looked.

"What's it for?" Pink asked.

"For the Illumination," Mackie said.

"What's that?"

"When my dad was a kid, the last Saturday of July was Illumination Night," Mackie said. "They used to decorate the harbor with the lanterns that the whaling captains had brought back from the Orient a hundred and fifty years ago. My dad doesn't know why they ever stopped the custom, but I've decided to revive it."

"You and your dad?" Pink asked. "You two are starting a committee?"

"Just me," Mackie said. "It was a kids' tradition. I plan to try to get a group together.

All the grown-ups are allowed to do is walk around Illumination Night and enjoy the show. I'm asking everyone to scrounge around their attics for lanterns the way I am."

"I never saw any lanterns in my folks' attic," Pink said.

"Well, if you look again, you might find one or two. Then you could lend them for the Illumination. Anyway, I was going to call you later about a photograph I found in the bottom of the trunk. Take a look."

Pink reached for the snapshot and moved closer to the light at the center of the attic so that he could see it better. It was a photo of two boys sitting on the steps of the Plymouth Island Courthouse, grinning at the camera. At first Pink was certain that the boys were Mackie and him. The photo could have been taken this summer, but the colors in it were faded and the paper was beginning to crack.

"It's weird," Pink said. "It could be us but it can't be us."

"Maybe we were friends in a previous life," Mackie said. He laughed but Pink didn't. He was a little upset by the resemblance. "It's got to be our dads," Mackie continued.

"But these two guys look like friends," Pink said. "My dad and your dad aren't particularly good friends and I never heard anything about them being friends when they were kids."

"They were both kids on Plymouth Island," Mackie said. "They must have known each other. I'm going to show it to my dad. If they were buddies, I'd like to hear about it."

"If they were, I'd like to know why they aren't buddies anymore," Pink said. "Wouldn't they at least talk about it?"

Both boys were quiet for a moment. Pink didn't know what Mackie was thinking, but he wondered if Mackie was thinking, as he was, that someday maybe the two of them wouldn't be best friends. Life could change like that. Next year, Pink knew, Mackie would be starting at Winslow, a New England boarding school. Mackie would be leaving the day school in New York where his family lived the rest of the year. Mackie's life would change and so might Mackie. As far as Pink knew, his life would always be Plymouth Island.

"If your committee needs an extra kid, I'm available," Pink said. "It would be fun to help out."

"Don't you have enough with your summer jobs?" Mackie asked. "I should probably get a job too. That way I'd have some money to get away from Winslow on weekends."

As usual, Mackie didn't sound happy about boarding school. He had talked about Winslow a lot with Pink, but as his time to go away to school there neared, his enthusiasm seemed to wane.

"You should be excited about going to a big-deal school like Winslow," Pink said. "It's supposed to be a terrific school. And it's going to be an experience, living away from home for the first time."

Mackie tried to smile. "I know I'm supposed to be excited but I'm just not, Pink. But my dad went there and it looks like I have no choice. Sometimes I wish I were you. I wish I could stay here on Plymouth Island all year and go to school here too."

"You might not like it all that much, Mackie."

"You like Plymouth Regional," Mackie said.

"Sure," Pink said. "But the school isn't much. Not like Winslow's going to be, I bet. There's no library. We do calisthenics in the cafeteria. It's not like we need a basketball court. We don't have enough guys to make up a team."

"You mean you don't like it?" Mackie asked.

"I guess I do," Pink said. "But that doesn't mean I wouldn't like someplace else just as much. Winslow's an opportunity for you. You should feel grateful."

Mackie's lips tightened. His voice was more tense. "Well, sometimes I just don't happen to feel what people tell me I'm supposed to feel."

"You sound like some poor little rich kid, Mackie." Pink couldn't believe he'd said that but he had.

"You're saying I'm a spoiled brat?" Mackie asked.

"I'm saying you sound like one is all," Pink said.

"Maybe I *am* a spoiled brat," Mackie said angrily.

"Maybe you *are!*" Pink responded, feeling angry himself.

Pink could see that he had only made Mackie feel worse, but he couldn't understand why Mackie wasn't looking forward to Winslow School. It was weird. Two days in a row he had found himself giving advice to friends. But what did he know about living on the mainland or going to a boarding school? It felt odd to find himself pushing Winslow and Mackie reacting so angrily. He took another look at the snapshot and hurriedly handed it back to Mackie. "You going to show it to your dad?" he asked.

"Unless you want to show it to your dad first," Mackie said. He still sounded annoyed.

"I'll keep it for a while," Pink said. "See what my dad has to say about it. I'm sorry about what I said before. I didn't mean anything by it."

"It's hard when someone tells me to be happy about something I'm not happy about," Mackie said. "When you were mad at Phoebe, I understood. I didn't tell you how you should feel. I like her okay but I know she can be kind of rotten."

"Well, I'm still mad at her," Pink said. "A little. I don't want to make a big deal out of it. You want to go sailing?"

"I'd rather stay in the attic," Mackie said.

"By yourself?"

Mackie nodded.

"You still mad at me?" Pink asked. Mackie was taking all this too far, he thought.

"Yes," Mackie said.

"I give up," Pink said. As he walked down the two flights of stairs, he couldn't believe that he and Mackie had had a fight. He hadn't been that pushy. Why did Mackie have to be hypersensitive? No matter how hard he tried, Pink didn't think he would ever understand why

Mackie wasn't willing to give Winslow more of a chance. How many kids ever got an opportunity like that?

As he walked out of the house, he saw Mr. Vanderbeck resting his bag of golf clubs in the trunk of a convertible. Mr. Vanderbeck had silver hair and a deep tan. He was as distinguished-looking a man as Pink had ever seen.

"Hi there, Pink," he said. "You and Mackie find any hidden treasure up there in the attic?"

Pink felt the snapshot in his pocket. He handed it to Mr. Vanderbeck. "Mackie found it," he said. "We thought it was us."

"But it's not," Mr. Vanderbeck said as he looked at it. "It's me and Charlie a long time ago."

"You look like friends there," Pink said.

"We were great pals," Mr. Vanderbeck said.

"Like me and Mackie?"

"It's a nice coincidence," Mr. Vanderbeck said.

"Did something happen?" Pink asked. "I mean you're not particularly good friends now."

"It's nothing for you boys to concern yourselves about," Mr. Vanderbeck said. "How is your dad, Pink?"

"He's fine."

"Send him my regards, will you?"

Pink nodded and got on his bike. As he pedaled toward home, he thought about his father's friendship with Mr. Vanderbeck. Mr. Vanderbeck had seemed deliberately vague about it.

The clock on the steeple of the Old Whalers' Church struck two. Pink decided not to worry about his father and Mr. Vanderbeck and pedaled faster. The clock reminded him that he had to get home before his mother did, before she had a chance to go through the mail. It was crucial that no one, his parents most of all, find out what he had sent away for.

4

PINK SPED through the traffic on Commercial Street and turned down Dock Street. As he approached the house, he skidded to a stop in front of the mailbox. It was empty. Pink felt a pang of anxiety. Was it one of those days when there was no mail for the Cunninghams? Could it be a holiday? It didn't matter which holiday, any day when the United States Post Office didn't deliver would do.

He leaned his bike against the shed and walked into the kitchen. His mother stood staring into the refrigerator.

"What you up to, Mom?" Pink asked. "Defrosting?"

"More like despairing," his mother said. "How does a leg of lamb, an apple pie, and an enormous salad sound to you?"

"Sounds like a great dinner," Pink said.

"I mean for an afternoon snack," his mother said. "We'll get to the heavy stuff when your father gets home from work."

Pink smiled as his mother started to re-arrange the inside of the refrigerator. She squeezed a jar of mayonnaise between two bottles of juice.

"Is today some kind of holiday?" he asked.

"If it were, I would have been the first one not to show up at the bank," his mother said. She slammed the refrigerator door shut and leaned against it to make sure it wouldn't open on its own. "You worked over at the boatyard this morning, didn't you?"

Pink nodded.

"Then it's no kind of holiday, Pink," his mother said. "What kind of mom lets her kid work on a holiday?"

"I just thought there might be a reason there wasn't any mail today," he said. He sat down at the kitchen table and picked a plum from the bowl of fruit on the lazy susan.

"There was mail," his mother said. "But not much. Maybe it's a very minor holiday no one bothered to tell us about."

"Anything for me?" he asked anxiously.

"You and I were the big losers," she said. "Not a thing for either one of us. Your father lucked out with some bills and something from that school that Mackie's going to in the fall. Can't imagine why anyone would send that sort of thing to him."

His mother picked up a brown envelope big enough for a pamphlet. She read the words on the upper left-hand corner, " 'Winslow School, Winslow, Massachusetts.' That's Mackie's school, isn't it?"

Pink stood up abruptly. "They sent it to Dad?" he asked.

"Says here 'Charles Cunningham.' Sorry, Pink. I didn't see the 'Jr.' How come they sent it to you? Mackie put you on the mailing list?"

She held out the envelope. Pink took it and tried to avoid the question mark on his mother's face. Maybe he should pretend to be as surprised as she was. He didn't want to lie to his mother but he wasn't ready yet to tell her the truth. So instead of doing either, he sat down again at the kitchen table and opened the envelope. He pulled out the catalog. The cover was a rich, deep blue. On the front were the words *Winslow School.* Underneath was a crest and some words in Latin, *Veritas et Fraternitas.*

"I guess it'll be interesting to look at," his mother said. "Too bad it's not the mail you've been expecting. You've been checking the mail every day for the last ten days," she said.

"The catalog's what I was expecting, Mom," he confessed. "I sent away for it." His voice was shaky but he was saying what he knew he should.

"You're upset."

"I was worrying you'd find it."

"Well, I found it," she said. "And the world didn't end. So why are you still worried?"

"I'm afraid of what you're thinking," he said.

"I'm thinking Winslow's a very fine school," his mother said. "Some of the brightest kids in the country go there."

"That's all you're thinking?"

"I think you're one of the brightest kids in the whole country," she said. "As far as I'm concerned, you are *the* brightest, but I'm your adoring mother so maybe I'm prejudiced. The trouble is that the parents of the kids who go to Winslow School are some of the richest parents in the world. You got the right brains, Pink, but it looks like you got the wrong parents."

"I've got perfect parents," Pink said.

"Okay," his mother said. "You've got perfect parents, but maybe if we had more money, we'd be even more perfect."

"That's not so," Pink said. "You can't improve on perfection."

"You wish you could go to Winslow?" his mother asked, becoming serious now. "Is that why you sent away for the catalog?"

"I was interested," Pink said. "That was all. Mackie talks about the school so much I couldn't help being curious. I knew I should have got to the mailbox before you did. I knew you'd be upset."

His mother poured herself a mug of coffee and sat down with Pink at the kitchen table. "You've got a right to send away for any catalog you want," she said, taking a sip of her coffee.

"But I don't want to make you feel bad," Pink said. "I know we're not rich like the Vanderbecks and it doesn't matter."

"Money makes a difference sometimes," his mother said.

Pink felt more and more uneasy. Usually his mother was full of jokes and wisecracks. It wasn't very often that he saw her so serious.

"It doesn't make a difference about how I feel about you and Dad," he said.

"I know that," she said. "It makes a difference about other things though. You sure that when you ordered that catalog, you weren't more interested in going to Winslow than you're letting on now?"

"But I can't go, Mom," he said. "So why even think about it?"

"You're the one who sent away for the catalog," she said. She took another sip from her mug but she kept looking at him. "Look, Pink. I'm not prying for my sake. It's just that you've got to be honest with yourself."

"What difference would it make even if I did want to go to Winslow?" he asked. "I couldn't do anything about it, except make myself miserable."

"I guess that's the trouble with being thirteen," she said gently. "You've got to learn to be realistic about what you think and feel even if there's nothing much you can do."

"Why?"

"It's part of growing up."

"Why didn't you tell me before?"

"I didn't want to spoil your childhood," she said, smiling.

Pink laughed along with his mother. He opened the catalog. On the first page was a photograph of a three-story brick building. At the center of the roof was a white cupola. To Pink's eye, the building wasn't particularly handsome, but it did look official, the way a place like Winslow School was supposed to look.

On the next page was a history of the school:

> *Since it was founded the year after the Civil War ended, Winslow School has turned out six generations of boys who have gone on to distinguish themselves and the School in government, industry, science, and the arts. Two have won a Nobel Prize, eleven have served in the Senate or the House of Representatives, and one has been a Supreme Court Justice. Two boys have become presidents of the United States.*

"That's heady stuff," his mother said. She was standing behind him now, reading what he had been reading. "Plymouth Regional has turned out a lot of good people, but it's a little short on Nobel Prize winners and Presidents of the United States," she said when she was finished.

"It's that they're rich and we're not," Pink said. "Those kids were born to it. They would have become whatever they became no matter where they went to school."

"You believe that's all there is to it?"

"I'm talking dumb, huh?"

"If you've decided that the reason you haven't won a Nobel Prize is because you go to Plymouth Regional, you're taking the easy way out."

"I'm thirteen, remember? They don't give Nobel Prizes to kids."

"Would you believe that every one of those Nobel Prize winners was thirteen once upon a time?"

Pink laughed. "Do I have to win a Nobel Prize, Mom?" he asked. "What if I grow up to be some minor brain surgeon or maybe a plain old millionaire? Wouldn't that be good enough for you?"

"Good enough for me doesn't necessarily mean good enough for you, Pink," she said.

His mother was making it tough for him again. Pink turned a few more pages while she continued to look over his shoulder. Toward the end of the catalog, at the bottom of one page, was a list of the expenses every Winslow boy needed to cover each year. There was room and board, tuition, plus school books and athletic fees.

Pink let out a whistle. A year at Winslow cost as much as a new car. It was more money than Pink had ever imagined school, any school or college, costing.

"Incredible," his mother said. "Your father will probably want to give you a short lecture on what the world is coming to when he sees that."

"I don't want to hear the lecture, Mom," Pink said.

His mother sighed. "Afraid he'll blow?"

"Afraid he'll think something's going on inside my head that shouldn't be going on," Pink said. "Do I have to show Dad the catalog?"

"You shouldn't be afraid to show him."

"But he'll get upset," Pink said. "I know he will. I guess I should have known you'd be cool but cool isn't Dad."

"I thought you were the kid with the perfect parents," his mother said.

She was trying to make a joke but it didn't make Pink feel any easier. He tucked the catalog in the hip pocket of his jeans and stepped outside.

It was getting late in the afternoon but his father wouldn't be back from the boatyard for another couple of hours. Pink decided to walk out to the lighthouse. Maybe he'd read some more of the catalog there. Maybe he'd think some more too, about the trouble with thirteen.

5

MACKIE? You want to go sailing this afternoon?"

Pink was standing at the kitchen counter with a sandwich in one hand and the phone in the other. He had painted a sloop all morning at his father's boatyard and he had already decided to put off going over to the Wilsons' for another day. Today Pink wanted to relax. He also wanted to straighten things out with Mackie, even though after reading more of the Winslow catalog the night before he wasn't sure that he was in the wrong.

"I guess sailing isn't in the cards for me this afternoon," Mackie said. "Sorry."

"How about some fishing?" Pink suggested. "I hear they're jumping at Pogue Sound. What do you say?"

"Not today," Mackie said.

"I'm sorry about yesterday," Pink said. "I'm sorry I got you riled up."

"Riled up isn't quite right. If I recall, you called me a spoiled brat," Mackie said.

"It was just the way you were talking."

"Just because I don't want to go to Winslow doesn't mean I'm wrong, Pink," he said.

"Come on Mackie, you're being too sensitive. You've talked about the school a lot and never got mad before," Pink said.

"Why do you care one way or the other how I feel about Winslow?"

"I don't know," Pink said honestly.

"Then don't tell me I'm being over-sensitive," Mackie said. "No one's making you go there. How would you know anything about what's going on inside my head?"

Pink could tell that Mackie was getting mad at him all over again. He had a feeling that if he listened to Mackie on the subject of Winslow School for one more moment, he would get mad too, although he wasn't quite sure why he was getting drawn in. "You want to change your mind about doing something with me this afternoon?" he asked, trying to change the subject.

"I got too much to do already," Mackie said.

"You want some help on the Illumination?" Pink asked.

"I don't think I need your help right now."

"Sure, Mackie," Pink said. "Maybe some other time, maybe when you've calmed down a little."

Pink said good-bye and hung up. The catalog was upstairs on his bed table where he had left it that morning. He picked it up and thumbed through it. When he came to the pages about the expenses, he quickly shut it, annoyed. How could Mackie not feel grateful?

Pink knew he should call up someone else. A beautiful Plymouth Island afternoon was no time to be alone. He thought of Derek Malloy, the guy whom Phoebe had dumped him for. Pink had nothing against him. In fact, he liked Derek. Derek was Pink's age and he had a summer job too. If he wasn't too busy taking ticket reservations at his grandmother's summer theater, he would be good for a visit. Derek didn't spend his time at the yacht club during the summer and in the winter he went to a regular public school. That made him more like real people as far as Pink was concerned and real people were what Pink needed right now.

At the Red Barn Theater, Pink got off his bike and rested it on the kickstand in the tar parking lot. He wandered over to the box office window and looked in.

Derek was by himself but he was on the phone. He noticed Pink and waved for him to come inside.

Derek had black hair, which Phoebe apparently liked better than red hair. But he spent so much time in the box office that he didn't have anything like Pink's tan.

"Hi there, Pink," Derek said as he hung up the phone.

Pink sat down in the wicker chair on the other side of the desk where Derek was sitting.

"You come here to buy some tickets?" Derek asked hopefully. "We're doing *Harvey.* It's a laugh riot."

"What's it about?" Pink asked.

"Well, it's about this rabbit. . . ."

"Sorry, Derek. I'm not into rabbit plays."

"I see your point," Derek said thoughtfully. "How's business with you?"

"Business?" Pink asked. "I'm not in business."

"You work, don't you?" Derek asked. "That's business."

"It's just work, Derek."

"Just work?" Derek asked.

"Caulking and painting in the morning,"

Pink said. "Raking a couple of afternoons a week. It's not worth talking about."

"It is for me," Derek said. "Maybe answering this phone doesn't look exciting to you, but it is to me. I love business."

"You love money," Pink said.

"You're so right," Derek said happily. "I figure I'm just getting into training for the future."

The telephone rang and Derek jumped for it before the first ring was over. He took a reservation for that night's performance and put down the receiver. Pink envied the look in Derek's eyes.

"I get tired of working," Pink said. "Don't you sometimes wish you didn't have to?"

"Have to?" Derek asked. "I want to."

"But don't you ever wish you were spending more time at the beach like the other kids?"

"Kids' stuff is for kids," Derek said. "Tans fade. Muscles go slack. Money is forever. At least my money is going to be forever. You know anything about blind trusts and CDs?"

Pink shook his head. He didn't feel like hearing about money, Derek's or Mackie's or Phoebe's, not today.

Derek put his feet on the desk and stretched his hands behind his neck. "You're getting to that age when you have to start planning for your future. Don't let your future happen without you. That's my motto."

"I'll keep that in mind," Pink said. "I'm a little young to get into that sort of stuff just yet."

Derek smiled patiently. He grabbed a pencil from the jar beside the phone and stuck the eraser in his mouth. Even though Derek was chewing it, Pink thought it made him look more serious. Maybe Derek thought so too. "Let me tell you something," Derek said. "When it comes to the future, there's no time like the present."

"I don't like that motto either," Pink said. "Do you want to start all over again?"

"Look, Pink," he said. "If I'm boring you, we could change the subject."

"Maybe we could *do* something this afternoon," Pink suggested.

"Unless you want to paint scenery, I got nothing to offer you, I'm afraid," Derek said.

"Sorry, Derek," Pink said. "I've painted enough hulls for one day.

Derek took his legs off the desk and leaned forward. "I know we're not exactly buddy-buddy, Pink, but may I ask you a question?"

"If it's not about blind trusts or CDs, shoot."

"Are you over Phoebe yet?" Derek asked.

"I don't need to get over her," Pink said.

"Are you sure?" Derek asked. "You're glum, Pink. It's not like you."

"She broke a date," Pink said. "That was all."

"Not your heart too?"

"The pain was closer to the area around my neck, Derek."

"The word around the island is that you're not accepting her apology," Derek said.

"I got my reasons," Pink said, though for the life of him, he wasn't exactly sure what those reasons were.

"Of course, it was lousy of her to break the date with you," Derek continued. "If I'd known she had invited you first, I would never have invited her to the dance at the yacht club. Even at twice the money Kit paid me."

"I appreciate that," Pink said. "I guess I don't want to hang around here after all. I'll find something else to do." Talking about Phoebe and the apology was making Pink anxious.

The telephone rang again. Derek picked it up. With his free hand, he got his pencil ready. "Red Barn Theater. Derek Malloy himself speaking. How may I serve you and yours?"

Derek nodded and frowned as he listened to

the person at the other end of the line. He sighed and put down his pencil. "Gee, thanks, but I don't see how I'm going to have time for that sort of thing. I'm swamped with my box office stuff. Maybe next year. Thanks, Mackie. Bye."

Derek put down the receiver and looked at Pink. "I guess that's something you already got out of," he said.

"I know you were talking to Mackie," Pink said. "But I don't know what you got out of."

"Mackie's asking all the regulars on the island to be on some Illumination Committee," Derek said. "They've got a meeting this afternoon. You've got to know about that."

Pink shook his head. He'd known Mackie was going to form a committee, but after his phone call this morning, Pink had assumed that Mackie hadn't started yet.

"Maybe Mackie couldn't reach you," Derek said. "He said he's been calling everyone he knows."

"Well, he didn't call me about it," Pink said.

"Don't worry about it," Derek said. "He must have tried to call. I mean if you're not a regular on this island, who is? Besides, he did say he was calling everyone, Pink, and everyone has to include you."

"I bet he didn't try to call Phoebe," Pink said.

Derek stuck the pencil back into his mouth. "I have a feeling he did call Phoebe," Derek said, very slowly.

"What makes you say that?"

"The first meeting of the Illumination Committee is over at the Wilsons' house," Derek said. "It starts in twenty minutes."

Before Derek could say another word, Pink was on his feet. He waved halfheartedly and walked to the parking lot. He wished he could believe that Mackie hadn't been able to get in touch with him, but the two of them had spoken only an hour before. How on earth could Mackie exclude him from the Illumination Committee? How on earth could he be friends with Phoebe when he knew Pink still hadn't accepted her apology? Pink didn't know whether he should be mad or hurt.

By the time he got on his bike, he realized that he was both.

6

WHEN PINK got to the corner of Commercial and Dock Streets, he decided he was more hurt than angry. It was bad enough when some girl dumped you, but a friend who dumped you was worse. How could Mackie not ask him to be on the Illumination Committee, he wondered. It didn't matter that the Illumination meant next to nothing to him. Nor did the argument they'd had matter, at least not to Pink. He had tried to make amends, but when he had offered to help out, Mackie had brushed his offer aside. By the time Pink was halfway down Dock Street, he could feel the anger taking the place of the hurt. How dare Mackie and Phoebe join up and exclude him?

He turned his bike around and started riding out of town. He pedaled so hard that it took half the usual time for him to get to the Wilsons' place. He was in too much of a hurry to use his kickstand. Instead, he sent his bike sprawling on the thick white gravel and strode up the front steps to the front door.

He knocked loudly three times before a middle-aged woman he'd never seen before walked down the front hall toward him. From what he'd seen in the movies and on television, he expected maids to look neat and tidy and walk briskly. This maid didn't. She was clean enough, Pink supposed, but her hair was a little on the messy side and her black uniform was wrinkled. It was the cigarette that surprised him the most. It seemed to be growing from the right side of the woman's mouth.

"You want something?" she asked as she opened the screen door a bit.

"I'm Pink Cunningham," Pink said. "I work outside a couple of afternoons a week."

"I've never seen you," the maid said. "On the other hand, I never go outside. Too much fresh air out there. Bad for my lungs. The name's Violet. Put 'er there, Pink."

She held out her right hand, which Pink shook quickly.

"I'm looking for Phoebe," Pink said. "She's around, isn't she?"

"She's in the living room," Violet said,

"but she's kind of busy. She's with the Vander-beck kid."

"That's fine," Pink said. "I'm here to see both of them."

Without waiting for Violet to move aside, Pink stepped into the hall. On the right was the living room. Sitting on the Oriental carpet in front of the fireplace were Phoebe and Mackie. All around them, on chairs and tables and on the sofa, were old lanterns. As Pink stepped into the room, they both looked up at him. Mackie started to scramble to his feet.

"Don't get up," Pink said. "I'm not staying."

"Then what are you doing here?" Phoebe asked.

"Where's the rest of your Illumination Committee?" Pink demanded.

"We're it," Phoebe said. "Everyone else was too busy."

"Are you sure?" Pink asked.

"That's what Mackie said," Phoebe said cautiously.

"Maybe Mackie didn't check with everyone," Pink said.

"Sure he did," Phoebe said. "Didn't you, Mackie?"

Mackie looked hesitant. "No," he said finally.

"I didn't ask Pink. I figured you were too busy," he added, almost apologetically.

"You didn't think I was too busy when you asked me to look in my folks' attic for lanterns," Pink said.

Mackie shrugged. "I figured you wouldn't be interested in being on the committee itself."

"Maybe you just didn't *want* me on your committee," Pink said. "You know very well that I offered to help this morning. Maybe it's something for summer people. Maybe you figure that year-rounders don't count."

"That's not true," Mackie said firmly.

"Phoebe here seems to think I don't count," Pink replied. His voice was rising now, but he couldn't help it. "You know how she treated me. How do you think your hanging around with her makes me feel?"

"She tried to apologize, Pink," Mackie said. "More than once."

"But I didn't accept," Pink said fiercely.

Now Phoebe was on her feet too and standing next to Mackie. "I know I was mean, Pink, and I still feel terrible about it," she said. "But if you're not going to accept my apology, that's more your problem than mine!"

"You're withdrawing your apology?" Pink asked.

"This is the last day I'm offering it," Phoebe said. "As of tomorrow, you can stew in your own juice."

"What's that supposed to mean?"

"It means I've suffered enough for my mistake," Phoebe declared. "It's time you started suffering for your own. I didn't dump you because you're a year-rounder. You have no right making me feel like a snob."

"Even if you are a snob?" Pink asked. "You summer people are all alike!"

Mackie took another step toward Pink. "You think I'm that way?" he asked. "It's nice to finally know how you really feel about me!"

Pink could hear the sarcasm in Mackie's voice but he was too angry to care. "If I'd started some committee, I would have asked you to be on it, Mackie. I would have asked you first."

"I'm sorry," Mackie said. "I'm really sorry."

"And if I had a chance to go to some fancy school like Winslow, you bet I would feel grateful and excited. You just take it for granted. I'm not supposed to tell you how you feel, but darn it, that's just how you ought to feel. It's not your fault maybe. It's the way you are. Both of you."

"It's the school, isn't it," Mackie said. "You don't care about the Illumination Committee. I bet you don't even care that much about Phoebe dumping you. You care about the school. You wish you could go, don't you? It's really us and what we have versus you and what you don't have."

Pink felt the blood rising to his face so fast that he was afraid he wouldn't be able to speak. "Watch it, Mackie!" he shouted. "You don't know what you're talking about. I don't care about that school. Plymouth Regional is fine by me. I'm happy there. And I'll be happier anywhere without the likes of you!"

"Well, no one's twisting your arm to stay *here*," Phoebe shouted at him.

Pink glowered at her for a moment before he realized that she was right. If he hadn't been so mad, he would have been embarrassed about shouting his lungs out in someone else's living room. "You're right, Phoebe, for once. I'm out of here!"

Without another word, he tore out of the living room and through the front hall. He couldn't believe Mackie dared to think he was jealous. How dare Mackie think any of it had to do with Winslow School?

As Pink pedaled on home, his breathing got

closer to something like normal. But even so, he felt himself getting madder and madder. "How dare Mackie?" rolled over and over in his mind. But for the moment, Pink couldn't dare to wonder if maybe Mackie was right.

7

PINK WAS still irate when he got home. He leaned his bike against the shed and strode past his father's office and through the boatyard. A couple of the men waved to him and Pink half-nodded. He was too full of his anger to talk to anyone.

What he needed was to be alone. Pink knew there was no place better for that than his skiff at the end of the boatyard's dock. It was barely large enough for two, but mostly Pink liked to sail in it by himself.

Pink jumped into the boat, adjusted the rudder, and raised the sail. Just as he reached for the ropes that tied the boat to the pier, he spotted a pair of feet on the wharf.

"You going someplace?"

Pink looked up. His father was holding the rope out for him to catch.

"I'm going for a sail," he muttered.

"No crew today?" his father asked.

"Today I'm captain and crew," Pink said.

"Can I be crew?"

"You got work, Dad."

"We haven't been out together all summer," his father said. "And I don't like the way you tore through the boatyard any more than I like the scowl on your face."

Mr. Cunningham didn't wait for Pink to invite him aboard. He stepped onto the boat and sat forward so Pink could sit in the stern. He was partially facing his father, but he turned as the wind caught the sail and the skiff started away from the dock. Soon they were sailing past the lighthouse and into the bay. A mile out to sea, thirty or forty sailboats were flocking toward the horizon. The sky was an almost cloudless blue and the sea was calm. Pink breathed deeply and exhaled. Some of the tension was leaving him.

They sailed in silence for a while until Pink saw that his father was staring at him. "You got something on your mind, Dad?" he asked.

"I want to know what's got you so worked up," his father said.

"I had a fight with Mackie and Phoebe," he said.

"Mostly with Phoebe, I hope," his father said.

"Mostly with Mackie."

"You two not on speaking terms?"

"We're on shouting terms is more like it," Pink said. "He started some dumb committee and then he got it into his dumb brain that I was upset because he didn't ask me to be on it."

"Why did he think that?"

"Because I threw a fit when I found out," Pink said, knowing he should laugh at himself, but not yet able to do that.

"You going to let it blow over?"

"I haven't decided," Pink said. "I don't know what to think so I'm not even going to try."

"I know how it is," his father said. "I was your age once."

Pink let the boat move to within a hundred yards of the sandbar that separated the bay from the sea then turned the skiff and sailed toward the harbor again.

"When you were my age, you were friends with Mackie's father, weren't you?" Pink asked. "How come you never told me?"

"It was a long time ago," his father said quietly.

"That's what Mr. Vanderbeck said to me," Pink said. "How come you stopped being pals, Dad? Was it because the Vanderbecks are summer people and we're not?"

"It was a long time ago," his father said.

"That's not an answer, Dad."

"Sorry, Pink," his father said. "It's better you take care of today."

Pink wondered why his father was as vague as Mr. Vanderbeck had been, but he didn't have time to wonder long. After a few minutes he brought the skiff back to the dock and his father hoisted himself out of the boat. When the sail was down and the rudder removed, Pink and his father walked back to the boatyard. The noise from the sawing and the hammering was deafening. Pink waved as his father turned toward his office. He was feeling calmer, but Pink didn't know if he was feeling better.

He went upstairs to his room, took off his sweater, and ran the brush through his hair. He noticed the snapshot of his father and Mr. Vanderbeck, which he had stuck in the corner of his mirror. Even if he didn't know what had happened between them, Pink couldn't help wondering if the same thing wasn't happening now between him and Mackie.

On the bureau was the Winslow catalog. Pink took the snapshot and tucked it into the back of the catalog. Idly, he took the catalog and lay down on his bed. He wasn't tired enough for a nap so he read instead. It was no big deal admitting that he was interested in the school, but that didn't mean he wanted to go there. If he didn't want to go there, how on earth could he be jealous of someone who could? It was ridiculous! Mackie was talking stupid. He had no right to talk like that.

Pink didn't know how long he read but soon he realized he was hungry. He hadn't heard his mother get home from the bank and when he got downstairs he was surprised that she was there. He was also surprised she wasn't staring into the refrigerator or slaving over a hot stove. One end of the kitchen floor was covered with old newspapers. On it were two cans of paint. One was orange. The other was green. His mother was kneeling beside the cans and dipping a brush into the can of orange paint.

"What are you up to, Mom?" he asked.

His mother turned and looked at him patiently. "I'm painting the kitchen," she said. "What did you think I was up to?"

"Just making sure," Pink said. "I thought you painted the kitchen last winter."

"I'm tired of yellow. It was a mistake to begin with."

"The Vanderbecks' kitchen is white," Pink said. "So is the Wilsons'."

"You prefer white?"

"It looks kind of elegant."

"Well, down here on Dock Street, we're not any kind of elegant," his mother said. "Why don't you eat a doughnut, dear. If you can eat a dozen before dinner, I'll raise your allowance."

Pink grabbed a box of doughnuts from the refrigerator and sat down at the kitchen table. He stuck one with chocolate icing into his mouth. He tried to rearrange himself in the chair to make himself more comfortable. But it was his seat rather than the chair's seat that was causing the problem. He pulled the catalog from his back pocket and set it on the table.

"You still reading that?" his mother asked.

"I haven't finished it yet," he said.

"It's not a novel," she said. "You don't have to finish it."

"You know they teach five different foreign languages at that school?" he asked. "And they've got a computer science course that's college level. It's incredible, Mom."

"And so is the tuition," his mother said. "I guess that's why I wish you would stop reading that catalog. I'm afraid not being able to go to a place like Winslow is going to depress you."

"It's okay, Mom," Pink said. "I know perfectly well there are things on the mainland we don't have here."

"But I don't want you feeling hurt for not having them," his mother said. She stood back from the wall to survey her work.

"Gosh, Mom," he said. "I'm just kind of interested. It's nothing more than that."

Pink stuck another doughnut in his mouth, more for his mother's sake than his appetite's. He opened the catalog to the page with the tuition expenses. He looked once again at the fees. They were every bit as high as the last time he had looked at that page.

He turned to the next page. There, at the top, were the words *Financial Aid.*

"They've got scholarships at the school," he said. "Did you know that, Mom?"

"I never thought about it," his mother said. "What's it say?"

"It's a list," Pink said. "Some of them cover the tuition and some of the others cover room and board. They're all named for the families that gave the scholarships. Here's a Katzenbach Scholarship and here's a deForest Scholarship. Here's one named for the Vanderbecks."

His mother leaned her brush against a can

of paint and stepped over to the table. "Well, we know the Vanderbecks have money," she said. "It's no secret."

" 'The Vanderbeck Scholarship is given each year to a boy of outstanding academic potential who might not otherwise be able to attend Winslow School,' " his mother read aloud. "And it looks like it's the only scholarship that covers everything: room and board and tuition."

"They can afford it," Pink said.

"But it's still nice of them," his mother said.

"Rich people do that so they won't feel guilty."

"You really believe that?"

"I'm just making a general observation is all," Pink said.

"Not all rich people feel guilty," his mother said. "Any more than they all have white kitchens. Mr. Vanderbeck apparently thinks you're a fine young man. He sent you a card when you were elected president of your class. If you're not getting an idea now, it's only a matter of time until you do."

"But there's more to going to a school like Winslow than the money," Pink said. "It means a change in everything. It means spending most of the year in some place you've never been before and with people you've never met."

"But if the money materialized from somewhere, a person could start to think about making those changes," his mother said.

"I live here," Pink protested. "What would you do without me? What would happen to the refrigerator?"

His mother reached across the table and took his hand. "I've been having this horrible feeling that someday you would double-cross me and grow up like everyone else's kid. I guess I don't like thinking about Winslow, but maybe it's time you started facing up to whatever you're feeling about the school."

Pink stood up and walked to the living room. He needed time to think now.

It was five o'clock by the small brass clock on the mantle over the fireplace. His mother wouldn't be starting dinner for another hour and they wouldn't be sitting down to eat for an hour after that. He still had plenty of time to ride his bike out to the lighthouse where he could be alone.

He looked at the catalog that was still in his hand. What his mother had said, maybe even what Mackie had said, was sticking in his mind and he needed to start figuring it out.

He dropped the catalog on the mantle and headed out.

8

I T WAS almost dark. Pink sat on the steps to
the lighthouse and waited for its enormous orange glow to fill the night. In the harbor, sailboats and yachts were at anchor. Pink could see
the lights in the portholes and hear laughter and
music from the boats.

His eyes followed the blue light on the stern
of the yacht club launch as it stopped at boat
after boat, picking up passengers and ferrying
them to the club. He heard a band warming up.
Tonight there was a dance at the yacht club.
Plymouth Island was in a festive mood but
Pink didn't feel part of it.

He rode home along the spit, hearing the
waves lapping below him. As he reached the
kitchen door, the light from the lighthouse went
on. He looked back at the harbor. It was as

beautiful as ever, but tonight the beauty didn't touch him.

"Pink? You there?"

"Yes, Mom. When's dinner?"

"Five minutes ago. It's cold soup and cold lobster. Get in here quick before it gets warm."

His mother and dad were at the table. Quickly he sat down and looked at his parents. Neither of them was eating. Both his parents were staring at him and neither looked particularly happy.

"What's up?" Pink asked as he rested his soupspoon in the bowl. "Anything wrong?"

"You tell me," his father said.

"I don't understand," Pink said. "What's happened?"

"Your father's upset," his mother said.

"Something down at the boatyard?"

"Something closer to home," his father said. "Something I found on the mantle when I was filling my pipe."

Pink shuddered. The Winslow catalog was lying in front of his father's soup bowl. "It's a catalog," Pink said. "That's all it is, Dad."

"Your mother says you sent away for the thing," his father said. He picked it up, thumbed through a few pages, and put it down again, closer to Pink's place. "How come you told your mother?" his father asked. "How come you didn't tell me?"

"Mom was home when it arrived," Pink said.

"You don't keep secrets from me," his father said. "It isn't like you, Pink. Were you trying to keep the catalog from me?"

"I was just interested in finding out more about that school," Pink said. "Mackie's going there in the fall. He talks about it a lot."

"Just because something's no big deal never kept you from talking about it before," his father said with a slight laugh in his voice.

"I didn't know how you'd feel about it, Dad," Pink said slowly. He took another spoonful of his soup. It tasted colder and more bitter than before. Pink hadn't done anything wrong. Why was his father making him feel as though he had?

He looked to his mother. She hadn't said anything yet and it didn't look as though she was about to say anything now. She collected the soup bowls and took them to the sink.

His mother passed him a plate. There was some lobster salad on it. After mariner's stew, lobster salad was his favorite food. Pink picked at it with his fork. He wondered if the trouble with thirteen had something to do with losing your appetite.

"I was thinking you probably wouldn't like it much, my sending away for the catalog," Pink said. "Maybe you'd think I wanted to go there. Winslow's a lot different from any plans we ever talked about."

"Well," his father said, "I always assumed you'd keep on at Plymouth Regional. Maybe go to the mainland for a couple of years of college. Come back here. Work with me at the boatyard. Just as I did with my father. That's about it, I guess."

"That's the way it always seemed to me," Pink agreed.

"You change your mind?" his father asked.

"Pink has the right to remain silent," his mother said. She wasn't smiling. "A boy's got a right to thoughts of his own. Thoughts he doesn't have to share with anyone, including two parents whom he worships and adores."

She offered the bread to Pink and then to his father. Both declined. His father wasn't about to let Pink's mother get in the way.

"You want to tell me what you're thinking, Pink?" his father asked.

"I wish I could go there, Dad," he said. It was as though a great burden had been lifted from him. He took a deep breath and exhaled slowly. All he had said was the truth, but it was the truth that had been gnawing away at him all summer. Only now was he able to say it, to accept it. "I guess Mackie was right. Maybe I am envious. I wish I could go to a school like that, a really fine school."

"I wish you could go too," his father said.

"You mean it?"

"You surprised?"

"A whole lot, I guess."

"A man wants the best for his kid," his father said. "Winslow School sounds like the best there is. I wish I hadn't read page forty-six. That's the only thing I'm sorry about."

"Page forty-six?"

"The page about the tuition," his father said.

"You didn't happen to read page forty-seven, did you?" Pink asked.

"What's on that page?"

"Maybe we should talk about it later," his mother said suddenly. "Haven't we had enough of the Winslow business for one day?"

"Tell me about page forty-seven, Pink."

"The Vanderbecks have a scholarship that sends a kid through Winslow," Pink explained. "Maybe I could apply for it, Dad."

"You're not applying for any scholarship that has anything to do with the Vanderbecks, Pink," his father said sternly.

"Why not, Dad?" Pink asked. "I bet I'm bright enough to get in. If Mr. Vanderbeck said I could have the scholarship, I could go."

Mr. Cunningham stuffed some tobacco into his pipe. He took a wooden match and struck it against the underside of the table. Pink wondered if his father was thinking or just delaying.

"You asked me the other day about Mr. Vanderbeck and me, so now I'll tell you," Mr. Cunningham said. "Henry and I used to be best of friends. All through our childhood, he used to come here every summer with his family just like Mackie does now. We were friends like you and Mackie 'til we got to be grown-ups. Then I made a big mistake. When I took over the boatyard from my father, there were a lot of problems. Money problems. I borrowed money from Henry Vanderbeck."

"And what happened?" Pink asked.

"We kept the boatyard," his mother said. "That's what happened. Pink, I knew your father still felt badly about the loan. I should never have let you think about the Vanderbeck Scholarship."

"How could I stop feeling that way?" Mr. Cunningham asked. "I lost my self-respect. I should have found the money someplace else."

"But aren't friends supposed to help each other?" Pink asked.

"I hated it," his father said. "As soon as he lent me the money, things changed between us. Taking the scholarship money would make you feel second-rate, Pink. It's lousy to feel beholden. It's a pity things work out that way but they do. It's up to us to show them we're just as good. Taking their money shows them we're not."

Pink heard the pain in his father's voice. Even if he didn't understand it all, he knew his father was trying to help him, not hurt him.

"If there were another way, I'd be all for your going to Winslow," his father said. "But I can't let you go through the frustration and disgrace I went through, Pink."

Pink nodded slowly, but he was so lost in his disappointment that he didn't hear the phone ring. Only when his mother was tapping him on the shoulder and pointing to the receiver did he come back to his senses. He stood and walked to the kitchen counter and picked up the phone.

"Yeah," Pink said.

"Pink? Can we talk about this afternoon?"

It was Mackie and he sounded friendly, not mad. Pink had planned to apologize the next time he spoke with Mackie. He had planned to admit that Mackie had been right. While sitting out by the lighthouse, he had decided that he was even going to ask Mackie about the Vanderbeck Scholarship.

"I know you're sorry," Pink said. "I'm sorry too. Other than that, I don't think there's much for us to talk about."

"We're friends, Pink. We've always got lots to talk about. How about some sailing tomorrow afternoon?"

"I won't be able to make it. Sorry."

"When can we get together?"

"I'm not sure."

"You still mad at me?"

"No," Pink said. "Honest. I shouldn't have been so mad at you in the first place."

"What's wrong, Pink?"

"We're different," Pink said. "Our families are so different. It was bound to get in the way."

He heard Mackie sigh.

"I don't believe you," Mackie said.

"I have to face it even if you can't," Pink said. "It would be easier if you did too."

As he put down the phone, he was sorry he had ever sent away for the Winslow catalog. Thinking he might go to a rich kids' school had been a terrible mistake. Getting to know rich kids had been another mistake. They only made you feel bad about the things you couldn't have.

From now on, Pink would know better. Mistakes like that hurt too much to make twice.

9

PINK TOSSED and turned all night. The next morning he felt exhausted. He dressed as usual in his jeans and T-shirt and brushed his hair. As usual, he checked the mirror to see if his hair was getting less pink. As far as he could tell, it wasn't. He guessed his hair was just another one of those things that was never going to change.

Pink looked again at the photo Mackie had given him. Just because Pink and Mackie looked like their fathers didn't mean things had to turn out the same for them. But the parallels were there and Pink couldn't ignore them.

If applying for the Vanderbeck Scholarship wasn't exactly the same thing as borrowing money, it was close enough. Pink stuck the photo in his pocket. Was what had happened to his father and Mackie's father bound to happen to him and Mackie? Pink wondered if it already had. Maybe that was what his conversation last night with Mackie had been about.

His mother had already left for the bank so Pink filled a bowl with cereal and ate it as he stood by the kitchen counter. Then he put on his sweater and walked over to the boatyard. Most of the men were already working.

Pink started working on the hull of an old wooden skiff. For the rest of the morning, he scraped and sanded. The din in the boatyard blocked thought and when the rest of the crew broke for lunch, Pink, as usual, was free for the rest of the day. He started thinking about the trouble with being thirteen, and the bad mood came on again. It was time to start figuring out who you were and what you wanted. He had been prepared to try, but now he had no choice but to listen to his father and try to understand.

While he fixed himself his lunch, he wondered what he should do that afternoon. One thing he wasn't going to do was spend another afternoon looking over the Winslow catalog. Another thing he wasn't going to do was work over at the Wilsons' place. Maybe now he owed Phoebe more of an apology than she owed him.

A day without Phoebe wouldn't do him any harm.

He thought of Derek. He got his bike from the shed and got on it. But, halfway to the Red Barn Theater, he remembered that his last visit to Derek had not been particularly helpful. He would skip Derek today too.

As he rode along the back street of Plymouth, he passed the Silvas' house. He hadn't seen Josh since the other day so he came to a stop and walked his bike up the Silvas' front path. Josh was hammering some nails into the porch steps.

"Hi, Josh," Pink said. "How's it going?"

"Pretty good," Josh said as he looked up and saw Pink. "Got chores today."

"Getting things ready for the new owners?"

"Keeping things safe for the old owners is more like it," Josh said as he took a nail from between his lips and began to hammer it into the wood.

"But you've got only a month 'til you move," Pink said. He remembered how, despite his attempt at encouragement, he had felt sorry for Josh for having to move to the mainland. Now Pink found himself envying Josh for going to school there.

"My mom and dad had second thoughts," Josh said. "Third, fourth, and fifth thoughts if you ask me. They decided not to move. They took the house off the market. My dad's real happy about it too."

"How about you, Josh?" Pink asked. "Are you happy about it?"

"I was trying so hard to be happy about moving to the mainland that it's a little hard to be happy about staying," Josh said. "I guess I'm sorry to miss some of those things on the mainland—shopping malls and schools with swimming pools and libraries crammed with books."

"I'm glad you're staying," Pink said. "That's for sure. Maybe it's all for the best."

"That's what you told me when we were moving to the mainland," Josh said. "Funny how we always say everything is for the best, no matter which way it goes. I guess you've just got to see it that way."

Josh went back to nailing the steps. "All for the best, all for the best," Pink muttered to himself. It wasn't so hard to say, but for Pink it was hard to believe.

"Mackie Vanderbeck is going to an expensive private school in the fall," Pink said. "And he wishes he could go to Plymouth Regional, just like we do. Isn't that something?"

Josh took the nails from his mouth and dropped them on the top step. Then he sat down next to the nails. "I guess the grass is always greener," Josh said. "Maybe I won't miss going to the mainland, but I'm sort of sorry not to have a chance to try it. It's having the chance that makes the difference, I suppose, more than the actual going."

"Maybe you're right," Pink said.

"Heck, it sounds crazy to you, I bet."

"You're not crazy, Josh," Pink said. "If you are, then I'm crazy too. I never thought of it that way, but it's the chance that makes the difference. Mackie doesn't have the chance to choose. Maybe that's what's getting him down."

"I never thought Mackie Vanderbeck and I had anything in common," Josh said. "I must be moving up in the world."

"Me too," Pink said.

"Huh?"

"You've just given me the answer I was looking for," Pink said.

Josh looked up at Pink. "I didn't know you were looking for the answer to anything," Josh said. "What's the question?"

As Pink got on his bike, he started to laugh. "I don't know what the question is either," he said. "But now that I have the answer, the question doesn't matter."

Pink knew he was on the right track now. He knew he had to speak to Mackie right away.

10

IT TOOK PINK fifteen minutes to ride out to the Vanderbecks' house and it took another five for Pink to find out that Mackie wasn't home.

"He's at the town wharf," Mr. Vanderbeck told him. "I assumed you'd be there too, Pink."

"What's going on?"

"Illumination preparations," Mr. Vanderbeck said. "I spent half the afternoon ferrying old lanterns down there."

On his way back, Pink detoured to his house. He wanted to check out the attic. He was in luck. What he was looking for was there. A few minutes later, he was riding his bike onto the town wharf. Here and there, clusters of tourists were taking snapshots. A few were sitting on benches, eating ice cream cones, and letting the sun work on their tans. Pink spotted Mackie in the shade of a shingled overhang. He was standing on a stepladder, attaching an elegant lavender lantern with black tassels to wire strung between several posts.

"You need some help?" Pink asked.

Mackie turned. "I sure do," he said. "My one and only committee co-member had an emergency."

"What went wrong with Phoebe?"

"She forgot she needed a new dress for tomorrow night," Mackie said. "She won't be back from the Teen Boutique for another hour. How'd you know I was here?"

"Your father told me," Pink said. "I went to your house looking for you."

"I'm glad you're here," Mackie said. "Could you hand me another lantern?" He pointed to a stack of lanterns lying near a piling.

"How about this one?" Pink asked. He held up the one he had found in his folks' attic. It was pink, but Pink liked it just the same.

"Thanks," Mackie said. He was smiling as he took hold of it.

"I'm here to apologize to you," Pink said.

"Then I accept," Mackie said nervously.

He kept his eyes on the lantern rather than on Pink.

"I should apologize for a lot of things," Pink said. "I'm not sure where to start."

"Start somewhere," Mackie said. "Apologies make me feel awkward."

"Then I'll apologize for making you feel awkward," Pink said. "How's that for starters? I'd also like to apologize for blowing up the other day. I had no right to get so mad at you for being friends with Phoebe."

"Apology accepted," Mackie said quickly. "We don't have to talk about it anymore, do we?"

"*I* have to," Pink said. "A little more." He picked out another lantern and held it out for Mackie. "I never told you I sent away for the Winslow catalog," Pink said. "I should have let you know that."

Mackie stepped down from the ladder and the boys sat down on the decking, their backs against a post, their faces in the sun.

"When did you do that?" Mackie asked.

"About a month ago," Pink admitted.

"It's nothing to apologize for."

"It's the sort of thing I shouldn't have kept a secret from you," Pink said.

"Why did you keep it a secret?"

"I was afraid you'd think I wanted to go there," Pink said. "I was afraid you'd feel sorry because I couldn't afford to go there."

"Do you want to go to Winslow?"

Pink knew the answer, but even so he hedged. He was still afraid. "I don't know enough about the place," he said. "I've heard you talk about it, which hasn't been too positive recently, and I've read the catalog backwards and forwards. But I've never even seen the place."

"Yeah, but do you want to go there?"

"I'd like to think I could go if I wanted to," Pink said. "That's probably it."

"I'm only going to ask you eleven more times, Pink," Mackie said. "Would you like to go to Winslow School?"

Pink caught his breath. "More than anything," he said heavily, painfully. It was even harder telling Mackie the truth than it had been saying it to his folks. "I want to go to Winslow. You happy now?"

"I'm dumbfounded."

"It's a great school, Mackie."

"And I bet you'd do great there," Mackie said. "A lot better than I will."

"It doesn't matter," Pink said. "Even if I passed the entrance exam, there are a lot of reasons I couldn't go. Heck. This is getting awkward for *me*. It's getting late too. I'd better be getting home."

Pink scrambled to his feet. What he'd intended to talk to Mackie about was impossible. Better to get out of there before he embarrassed himself and Mackie.

"It's the money, isn't it?" Mackie asked. "Pure and simple. There aren't a lot of reasons. There's just one."

"It's an excellent reason though," Pink said.

"I'm sorry."

"I'm sorry I was jealous of you," Pink said. "That's something else I need to apologize for."

"Then maybe I need to apologize for not being very sensitive," Mackie said. "Hearing me complain about having to go there must have been rough for you. You want me to talk to my dad about the Vanderbeck Scholarship?"

"How'd you guess?"

"I read the back of the catalog too," Mackie said, laughing.

"My dad says I'm not even allowed to think about that," Pink said. "My dad finally told me what happened. He and your dad were great friends when they were our age, Mackie. But then my dad borrowed money from your dad and they weren't friends anymore. My dad says the scholarship is like borrowing money."

"My dad thinks a lot of you, Pink," Mackie said. "I could talk to him about it tonight. Even if I don't get a choice about Winslow, I hope you do."

"I'd have to tell my dad," Pink said. "I don't know when I've had to tell him anything harder, but I want that chance. You talk to your dad and I'll talk to mine. I may need your dad to pacify mine."

"Who knows?" Mackie asked. "Maybe it could even get them to be friends again."

"You're a good friend," Pink said. "Let's stay good friends. Let's not let history repeat itself."

Pink got on his bike. The sun was dipping toward the horizon and he had to get himself home, get himself prepared to tell his father what he had done.

It could happen, he thought. Maybe. Probably. Probably not. No way. As he rode home, he still couldn't see it working out. But, even if his father blew, Pink knew he had to try. That was the answer he had been looking for all along.

11

HIS FATHER was working late again in his office at the boatyard and for once his mother wasn't holding dinner any longer. She had sent Pink to get him. If Charlie Cunningham wasn't about to come willingly, Pink had his mother's permission to drag him home.

Pink stepped into the office. In one corner was the wood-burning stove that heated the place in the winter. A half-dozen soundings maps were thumbtacked to the rough, unfinished walls. Hanging from the opposite wall were the lobster traps, oars, and small anchors that had been collected over the years.

At the far end of the room, Mr. Cunningham was working on his accounts under the light of the brass lamp with the green glass shade. In the evening, Pink wasn't so aware of the clutter of papers, ashtrays and styrofoam cups. To Charlie Cunningham, a tidy office didn't look like a working office.

Pink rapped twice on the door frame, but his father didn't look up. Then he cleared his throat. "Mom says dinner's ready," he said. "She means business, Dad."

Mr. Cunningham looked up. "I guess I could eat," he said. "You must be starved. It's almost eight."

Pink wasn't even hungry. Since he had spoken to Mackie, he had dreaded dinner. Soon he would have to tell his father that Mackie was talking to Mr. Vanderbeck about the scholarship. He took a breath and decided the sooner the better.

"Dad, there's something I've got to tell you," he said.

Mr. Cunningham stood up. "Tell me at dinner," he said.

"I'd like to tell you now," Pink said. "Before we eat."

"Man-to-man stuff, huh?"

Pink nodded slowly. He was about to open his mouth when the phone rang. Mr. Cunningham picked it up, listened for a second, and handed the receiver to Pink.

"Yes?" Pink said into the mouthpiece.

"Gosh, I'm glad I got you," Mackie said breathlessly at the other end. "I tried your house and your mom said to try the boatyard."

"Where's the fire?" Pink asked. "You sound weird."

"The fire's going to be at your house and it's going to happen very soon," Mackie said excitedly. "I just told my father about your wanting the scholarship and he was really pleased. But when I told him about your father not letting you apply for it, he blew. He stormed out of the house and drove off. I think he's on his way to your house and I don't think he's going to help you pacify your dad. I've never seen him so mad, Pink!"

"Did he say anything?"

"He was in too much of a rage to speak!" Mackie said.

Outside there was a screech of brakes so loud that even Mackie on the other end of the line heard it. "I think you have a guest," he said. "Don't say I didn't warn you."

As Pink hung up the phone, the door behind him slammed. There was Mackie's father, and behind him was Pink's mother. Pink had never seen Mr. Vanderbeck so mad or his mother so worried.

"Henry?" Pink's father asked. He was on his feet and looking more pained than Pink could ever remember.

"I've got to see you, Charlie," Mr. Vanderbeck said. "I hear Pink wants a crack at Winslow and you're not letting him go for it."

"Pink, go back to the house," Mr. Cunningham said. "You too Maggie."

"You bet," Pink said, happy at the prospect of being anywhere but in that room.

"The boy should stay, and so should his mother," Mr. Vanderbeck said. "What I'm here for has to do with Pink."

"I don't want to hear a word from you, Henry," Pink's father said. "Pink's not taking any Vanderbeck money and that's that."

Pink's mother took his father's hand. "Please, Charlie," she said. "Hear him out."

"And then you can kick me out," Mr. Vanderbeck said. "Pink wants to go to Winslow. I can help him. The Vanderbeck Scholarship is there for a bright, worthy kid and Pink qualifies as best I can tell."

"You're not doing us any favors," Charlie Cunningham said. "No matter what you think."

"It's a way for Pink to get the best education he can," his mother said. "It's a favor other boys would be happy to live with."

Pink didn't know what to say but he had a feeling that he ought to say something. Three adults were talking about his future as though he wasn't even in the room. "My dad says I'll think less of myself if I take the scholarship," Pink murmured. "He says it's like the money you loaned him."

"Pink, please," his father said. "We're talking about you."

"Maybe we're not," Pink's mother said. "Aren't we talking about something that happened before Pink was even born?"

"The fact is we don't need any Vanderbeck charity," Mr. Cunningham said. "Even if we did, we wouldn't take it."

Mr. Vanderbeck's mood was not improving. Pink could see that his deep tan was turning somewhat red. "It had nothing to do with charity," he exclaimed. "It was a loan. You paid it back, Charlie, and with interest too. It was a business deal between friends. If I had known how you would feel, I never would have offered it to you. But I respected your feelings, even though they cost me a friendship. But I'm not about to let your pigheadedness get in the way this time around. When Mackie told me about your standing in the way of Pink's getting the education he deserves, I saw red, Charlie."

"I don't want to talk about it anymore," Mr. Cunningham said. "Good evening, Henry."

"You were ashamed," Mr. Vanderbeck continued. "You had no right to feel that way and you let it create a gulf. Don't let that happen to Pink and Mackie. The Vanderbeck Scholarship isn't a handout. It's an opportunity. It's an investment. The difference is that Pink can pay it back by becoming all the things he can be. Maybe someday he could help another kid like him."

"Pink doesn't want it," Mr. Cunningham said. "I'll thank you and your son to stay out of the Cunninghams' business from now on."

Pink took a deep breath. He knew it was time for him to speak up. "I made it the Vanderbecks' business, Dad," he said slowly. "I asked Mackie to talk to Mr. Vanderbeck about the scholarship."

"But that was before I explained things to you, son," Mr. Cunningham said.

"No, Dad. It was after."

Mr. Cunningham looked stunned. "But you said you understood."

"I understood all of it, Dad, except why I shouldn't have a chance of my own," Pink said. "I'm sorry about what's happened to you and Mr. Vanderbeck. And I'm sorry I didn't tell you about changing my mind before I went to

Mackie. I would have explained it tonight if Mr. Vanderbeck hadn't showed up. But I want to make that chance for myself, Dad. I want the chance to choose my own life."

"It means that much to you?" Mr. Cunningham asked slowly.

Pink nodded.

"I didn't know," Mr. Cunningham said sadly. His shoulders dropped.

"You've always been pigheaded about this, Charlie," Mr. Vanderbeck said. "When you get into that 'I'm-not-as-good-as-you nonsense,' you stick with it come hell or high water."

"Maybe you're right," Mr. Cunningham said. "Pink, you've got a say in your own life. It's not for me to decree what you can't do, though I can't promise I'll be quiet when I don't like it."

Pink looked from his father to Mr. Vanderbeck and then to his mother. His father looked worried, Mr. Vanderbeck looked pleased, and his mother wasn't giving the slightest hint as to how she was feeling. Pink guessed it meant he could give Winslow a shot if he wanted.

But still, he wanted to ask each one for an answer. He started to speak, then stopped. They didn't have the answers for him now. He had to start looking for them on his own. Then he realized he'd already begun.

12

THE GULLS were soaring and swooping above the waves in the harbor. Their antics were as comical as ever but Pink wasn't paying attention. In the twilight, his interest was focused on the town wharf, all lit up with Japanese lanterns.

Crowds promenaded up and down, savoring the occasion. It was one festivity that summer people and year-rounders could enjoy together.

"Pink?"

He turned to see Phoebe skipping down the street toward him. She was wearing her new dress, earrings, and even a little make-up.

Pink thought she had never looked prettier.

"Hi, Phoebe," he said. "How are you doing?"

"I'm doing fine," she said. "What do you think of the Illumination?"

"It's sensational," he said. "You and Mackie did great. Congratulations."

"I wanted to congratulate you too," she said.

"I'm not ready for congratulations," he said. "Not yet at least, but thanks."

"But I heard you're leaving the Island tomorrow," she said. "You're going off to Winslow."

"My mom and dad are taking me there for a look around," he said. "I'll be taking the entrance exams too. If I don't pass them, I won't get in. If I do pass, I still might not go. I'll see how I feel."

"You mean you won't know until you know?" Phoebe asked.

"That's what it boils down to, I guess."

They were walking toward the harbor now. It was the last day of July, but the Island was so glorious that Pink couldn't get very intense about the decisions he would have to make.

"I guess I wanted to go partly because I thought it would make me as good as people like you, Phoebe."

"Don't say that. It's embarrassing."

"But it's true. And then I didn't want to

go because I knew it would make my dad feel bad."

"How does he feel now?"

"It's hard for him," Pink admitted.

"Is he making it hard for you?"

"You bet he is," Pink said, "but he says I have to make up my own mind and that's not easy. I probably owe you an apology, Phoebe."

"I'd hoped we were through with the apology business for this summer," she said.

"It's a deal," he said.

He held out his hand to her and they began to walk through the crowd. He wondered if maybe Phoebe would go sailing with him in his skiff. He didn't know what would happen about Phoebe or Winslow or anything else. But for now he was happy to be where he was, and for the first time in a long time Pink was happy to be who he was.